FIRST DEER CHEER

First Deer Cheer © 2021 by Kevin Lovegreen.
All rights reserved. No part of this book may be reproduced
in any form whatsoever, by photography or xerography or by
any other means, by broadcast or transmission, by translation
into any kind of language, nor by recording electronically or
otherwise, without permission in writing from the author,
except by a reviewer, who may quote brief passages in critical
articles or reviews.

Cover Illustration by Margarita Sikorskaia

Softcover ISBN 13: 978-1-7346743-9-2
Hardcover ISBN 13: 978-1-7370808-0-0

Printed in the United States of America

Cover and interior design by James Monroe Design, LLC.

Lucky Luke, LLC.
4335 Matthew Court
Eagan, Minnesota 55123

www.KevinLovegreen.com
Quantity discounts available!

Chapter 1

I lean over in the back seat so I can see between my dad and Greg. Through the bug-plastered windshield of Dad's truck, I see the headlights bounce up and down. We're turning onto the old dirt driveway, which marks the end of our four-hour journey.

Then I see it. Grandma and Grandpa's magical old red log cabin. It's tucked way back in the woods of northern Minnesota. The truck headlights shine on it like a spotlight shines on a star on stage.

"There she is, Crystal," Dad says. "Just sitting there, waiting patiently for us to return."

"Yep. And I can't wait to get inside!" I say.

We have been coming up here my whole life. We've spent a million hours swimming in the lake at the bottom of the hill. Animals and birds are everywhere, which is cool. The adventures never end up here in the woods.

And this will be the best weekend ever! It's the youth deer season. It's a special time when young hunters like me can go after whitetail deer before the regular hunting season begins in a few weeks.

I look over at the seat next to me. Megan is curled up on a pillow pressed against the window. She's been sleeping for hours.

"Megan, wake up! We're here!" I say, unable to contain my excitement.

Megan is my best friend in the whole world. We have known each other since kindergarten. She always has a sparkle in her eye and a smile on her face—when she's not tired, that is.

We both play volleyball and softball. We're always on the same teams. (But I'll admit she's a little better than me!)

The coolest thing, though, is that we both love shooting guns and hunting!

Greg is Megan's dad. He and my dad have become friends over the years, especially because they love hunting and the outdoors too. They've been showing us girls how to shoot guns since we were ten.

That's why this weekend is so special. Because we're twelve, Megan and I get to hunt deer with our dads for the first time!

For a few years now, I've gone out several times to sit with Dad while he hunts. But tomorrow is the first time I will have the gun in my hands. I can't wait!

I'm not sure who's more excited: us girls or our dads. Dad and Greg have been acting a little crazy the last two weeks. They've been talking on the phone constantly and going through all the details with us girls. My dad never got me this ready for any volleyball game, I will tell you.

Dad even decided to leave my little brother, Luke, home this weekend. That way, Dad and I can spend the whole weekend together. It killed Luke to stay home. He loves hunting and coming to the cabin as much as I do. But that little dude will have plenty of time to join Dad and me on other hunts when he gets older!

Megan and I are so lucky that our dads take us hunting. We have friends at school who think hunting is only for boys. That's crazy, I tell them! Girls love hunting too. No different than boys. Whether you're a girl or a boy, all you need is someone to help you learn how to do it, so you can get out there and give it a try. And that's exactly what Megan and I are going to do this weekend!

I look at Megan again. She's *still* sleeping.

"Megan!" I repeat, shaking her this time. "We're here!"

"What? Huh? Are we there yet?" she says through a frog voice. She pushes her shoulder-length brown hair out of her face as she slowly comes back to life.

"Yes! We're here!"

"Welcome back to the land of the living, Megan Marie!" Greg says in a funny high-pitched voice from the front passenger seat.

Greg is always joking around. He's about the same height as my dad but bigger. Let's put it this way: if they played on the same football team, Greg would be a lineman, and my dad would be the quarterback.

Greg has dark-brown hair like Megan, and my dad has strawberry-blond hair like me. It's kind of funny, now that I think about it. I guess that's how it works sometimes.

Dad pulls the truck up to the cabin and cuts the engine. "We made it!" he says with a proud smile.

"Never a doubt," Greg says as he opens his door and slides out.

I unbuckle, pull on my favorite green volleyball jacket, and open the door. Instantly, the cold October air hits my face. I love it! I take a big breath in through my nose. A smile fills my face as the familiar smell of fresh pine is everywhere.

Instantly, I'm right at home. I love everything about the north woods and this cabin.

Dad makes his way inside the cabin and turns on the porch light. Like magic, the whole yard lights up.

I grab my blue duffel bag and head inside too. There's no need to take off our shoes as we enter. The old brown linoleum floor can hold up to whatever we drag in from the outside.

Dad is busy lighting the big black barrel stove just outside the kitchen. It's not crazy cold here inside the cabin, but we could definitely use some heat. Greg goes through the doorway that is just off the kitchen and heads to the living room to light the fireplace there as well.

I make my way over to the two little beds that sit just off the kitchen. That's where Megan and I will sleep. The dark brown wood-paneled walls are filled with outdoor pictures and a huge mounted northern pike my grandpa caught years ago.

Still looking half asleep, Megan comes in, lugging her pink camo bag over her right shoulder. She drops the bag with a thud on the floor.

"I'm *tirrred*, Crystal . . ." she says, dragging out her words.

"I'm too excited to be tired," I reply. "We're going hunting in the morning!"

Megan nods and forces a half smile. Without a word, she turns to go outside to get another load from the truck.

I can't help but laugh. I know she's just as excited as me. We've been talking about this for weeks. But one thing about Megan is that she likes her sleep!

Before we know it, the truck is unloaded. Inside, the stove is warming up the kitchen and the main area of the cabin. Greg also has the fireplace roaring in the living room. The light from the flames are dancing on the walls.

The living room is my favorite place in the cabin. It has green carpet and a bunch of windows looking down the hill to the lake. The fireplace fills up the wall on one end, and it always keeps us warm.

On the back wall, there is a giant picture frame packed full of photos. Most of the pictures show someone posing with an

animal from a hunt or with a fish they've caught. In one picture, my great-grandma and great-grandpa look really young. They're holding up a stringer of northern pike they caught.

Above the picture frame, the wall is filled with deer antlers from the forty years the cabin has been in the family. Each set of antlers has a story to go with it.

I love hearing Dad share their stories of past hunts. When Dad tells his tales, he sometimes gets so excited that he stands up with his hands going crazy.

I can't believe tomorrow will be the start of *my* hunting stories.

"OK, girls," Dad says, herding us out of the living room. "It's late, and we gotta get up early. Let's get your clothes laid out so you'll be ready to go in the morning."

Dad and Greg both follow us to our beds as we open up our duffel bags.

"Let's see what you have," Dad says like an inspector.

I start pulling stuff out of my bag. "Socks, long underwear, my long-sleeve volleyball shirt, my volleyball sweatshirt, my volleyball sweatpants, gloves, and snow boots."

Megan sorts through her bag. "I have all the same stuff—except for long underwear," she adds. She pulls out her volleyball gear, which is identical to mine.

Greg raises his eyebrows. "Well, thank goodness for volleyball, otherwise you girls would be out there in your pj's!"

Dad goes out to the coat rack in the mudroom. It's full of jackets and gear, mostly from all the hunters over the years. He comes back with two blaze-orange jackets and stocking caps.

"Here you go, Crystal," he says, handing me one of the jackets. "You get to wear your grandma's jacket. She got this when Grandma and Grandpa first got married. Oh, if this jacket could tell stories, that would be fun."

He turns next to Megan. "And you can wear this jacket. Hmm . . . not sure whose it is. It looks like it'll be kinda big on you, but it will work!" Dad laughs as he tosses Megan the jacket.

"And these hats should work," he adds, giving us each one. "The rules say we need to wear an orange hat and jacket when in the woods during hunting season. It helps everyone stay safe," he informs us.

"We're gonna be stylin', Crystal!" Megan says as she pulls on the orange stocking cap. She gives us a double thumbs-up and the proud smile she uses all the time. "Orange is my color!"

Greg smiles and shakes his head. "You can sleep in the hat if you want. Either way, you girls better hit the hay."

Megan and I say good night to our dads, then crawl into our sleeping bags. It takes Megan about two seconds to fall asleep. I don't know how she does it!

As for me, I still feel too amped up to sleep. I close my eyes, hoping to count some sheep. Instead, I picture a bunch of deer walking through the woods, right to our stand.

Oh, man! I can't wait for tomorrow morning—which means this will be a long night!

Chapter 2

"Good morning, girls."

I hear these words muffled through a deep sleep. It sounds like Dad's voice.

This can't be real. This has to be a dream! It seems like I closed my eyes just seconds ago. How did I ever fall asleep? And how could it possibly be time to wake up already?

Then it comes again.

"Good morning!"

My eyes slowly open, and I realize I'm not dreaming. Dad is calling to us from the kitchen.

I look over at Megan. Her head is under her sleeping bag. I reach over and give her a double tap on her head.

Like a butterfly coming out of a cocoon, she emerges. Keeping one eye closed, she peeks at me with the other.

"This can't be happening," she groans. "Didn't we just go to bed?"

"I thought the same thing!" I reply.

Squinting at the old wood clock on the wall, I see the hands are at 5:45. Oh boy, it's early!

Even though I'd give anything to curl back into my sleeping bag, I force myself to slowly sit up. And then it hits me. This isn't just any morning.

It's opening morning of the youth deer season.

It's finally here! We get to go hunting! I manage to crack a tight smile.

Megan and I dress, then head over to the kitchen table. Dad has cereal, milk, and sugar donuts sitting out.

"Good morning, Dad," I say.

"Good morning, Sunshine! Are you ready to have some fun?"

"Yep!" My smile is getting bigger and bigger.

"Let's just have a light breakfast now," Dad says. "When we come back later, we'll have bacon and eggs!"

Greg makes his way into the kitchen too. "Would a cup of hot chocolate help wake you girls up?" he asks.

"It wouldn't hurt," Megan says.

I nod my head up and down, agreeing with Megan.

As Greg heats up some water, Megan and I chomp on donuts.

"Why'd we have to get up so early?" Megan asks with her mouth still full.

"Because we need enough time to get ready and get out to our stands before the legal shooting time begins," Dad explains. "We can shoot a half hour before sunrise, which is pretty early. And we want to sneak into our stands before the deer can see us. So that all adds up to us getting up before the crack of dawn."

"Oh, man," Megan says looking at me. "That's a lot of information this early."

"You just relax, Megan Marie. We got this." Greg then turns to Dad. "So, what time is sunrise this morning?"

Dad grabs his phone. "Hey, Google—what time is sunrise?"

"Today, the sun will rise at 7:40 a.m.," the Google voice says.

Greg shakes his head. "What did we do before smartphones?"

"So that means we can legally shoot at 7:10," Dad calculates. "I want to be in our stand a little before seven. So, we should roll out of here at six thirty. That gives us twenty minutes to eat up and get our gear on."

"Sounds like a plan," Greg says. "OK, Megan Marie—turn it up a notch!"

After some hot chocolate and another donut, Megan and I scurry to get our hunting clothes on. For the finishing touch, we both pull on our stocking caps and high-five. We agree that we look ready.

The dads have our cased guns, shells, and backpacks. Out the door we go.

Considering that it's well before sunrise, it isn't as dark out as I thought it would be. I look up and there it is—a full moon as big as life.

"Whoa, look at that moon!" I exclaim, pointing up in the sky.

Megan follows my finger. "That's cool! And look at all those stars. There are billions of them. We don't have that many at home."

"Actually," Greg says, "we have this many stars above us at home too. But we just can't see them because we live in a metropolitan area—a city. There's so much light in a city that it dulls the sky. Out here, though, there are hardly any lights at all. That's why you can get amazing views like this."

After staring at the moon and stars for a few seconds, we all pile into the truck for the short ride to our hunting land.

"We won't even need our headlights," Dad says. "The moon will give us plenty of light to find our way."

Dad takes off, and the truck bounces down the driveway. I feel my smile grow so big I can barely contain it.

This is it! Hunting, here we come!

Chapter 3

When we arrive at our magical hunting property, Dad pulls off to the side of the road.

"You guys jump out here," he says to Greg and Megan. "With a light west wind, Vern's Stand should be perfect for you."

Vern is my uncle—Dad's brother. And of course, the tree stand he built and loves to hunt out of is named Vern's Stand. There are a number of stands on the property, and they all have names. There's Jerry's Stand, The Y, The Pine Tree Stand, and more.

"Vern's Stand sounds good to me," Greg replies. "Come on, Megan. Let's roll."

"Good luck, Megan!" Dad says. "Have fun out there."

"Thanks! I'm sure I will."

As she gets out of the truck, Megan turns and gives me a thumbs-up. "Good luck! Get a big one!" she adds in a deep voice to emphasize her point.

"You too!" I say in a deep voice, but mine isn't all that convincing.

We break out laughing.

"Shh!" Dad shushes. "We don't want to scare all the deer away."

Megan quickly covers her mouth and looks guilty. "Sorry," she whispers through her hand. "Sometimes I just can't help myself!"

Dad and Greg smile and shake their heads at us. What would they do without us girls? They wouldn't have any entertainment! That's the way I see it.

Once Greg and Megan are on their way to Vern's Stand, Dad pulls away.

"Which stand are we going to?" I ask him.

"My stand," he says. When he looks back at me through the rearview mirror, I see his eyes light up.

My eyes light up too. Dad has shot a bunch of deer from his stand. Each time

I have sat with him, we have seen deer. I can't wait!

We drive slowly down the dirt road, take a right turn at the corner, then drive for a little while more. Finally, Dad pulls to the side of the road and puts the truck in park.

"We'll walk in from here," he says. "But first, let's go over a few rules."

I nod and sit up a little straighter.

"In our area, you kids can shoot only a doe during the youth deer season," Dad says. "And you know how to tell the difference, right?"

"Does don't have antlers, like bucks do, silly. Of course I know that."

"Right. So we're going to look for the right doe to take. Hopefully, we can find a nice big one that doesn't have a fawn with her."

"Got it. Does are better eating anyway," I say.

Dad looks back at me with a crinkled face. "Sounds like you've been listening to your mother."

"Yep!"

Dad grins. "You're a hoot! Now, let's get to the stand!"

Dad pulls my .243 rifle out of the case, then hands it to me. I check the safety and open the bolt to make sure it doesn't have any bullets in it. Then I close the bolt and sling the rifle over my shoulder.

"Very impressive, young lady. You've got great gun-safety skills."

With a proud smile, I follow Dad into the woods.

Megan and I both have .243s. Mine has a camo pattern with beautiful leaves. Megan's is pink camo, which is typical for her. She loves pink.

As we walk, I'm once again thankful for that full moon. My eyes start to adjust, and I can see pretty well. My favorite part is that the moon is so bright that it casts our shadows, just like the sun does during the day! That's pretty cool.

The walk is taking longer than I expected. The trail is straight through the thick woods. Even with all the moonlight, it's still kinda spooky.

I'm sure glad I'm walking with Dad. There's no way I would be doing this alone. With Dad, though, I can do just about anything.

We finally take a right off the trail and head deeper into the woods. I can see the deer stand ladder just in front of us. Dad's stand is all wood. He said his dad, my grandpa, showed him how to build it.

I never met my grandpa. He died before I was born. But over the years, Dad has told me many stories about Grandpa and how much he loved hunting and this land.

I don't think about Grandpa often, but for some reason, I'm thinking about him now. I bet he would be super excited to know his granddaughter is out hunting.

Maybe he'll bring us some luck today. Who knows!

Dad takes my gun and sends me up the ladder first. I climb slowly, making sure my feet hit every rung. Then I crawl under the railing and sit on the bench seat.

When Dad gets to the top of the ladder, he carefully hands me my gun. Then he slides off the backpack and sets it along the edge. After all that, he finally crawls and wiggles his way in. He's not as smooth as I was, but he makes it.

Dad and I are shoulder to shoulder. We have to get pretty cozy up here—there's just enough room for Dad, me, and the backpack.

Dad takes my gun back and pushes three shells in. He then slides the bolt forward, sending a very loud and unnatural sound into the woods. Dad winces and raises his shoulders, like he got zapped.

"That was louder than I thought it would be," he whispers.

I cover my mouth so I don't laugh.

Moving slowly and quietly now, Dad hands me my gun. "The safety is on, and she's ready to go."

I nod and give him a thumbs-up. Just to be sure, though, I double-check the safety. That's what Dad taught me: every time you pick up a gun, you check the safety. Even if someone tells you the safety is on, you *must* check it yourself. It's one of the many safety rules Dad has instilled in me.

I draw in a big, deep breath.

I'm hunting! Bring on the deer!

Chapter 4

We sit in the moonlight that peacefully fills every gap in the woods. It's so quiet I can hear my own heart beating. I can feel steam escaping from inside my jacket and hitting my neck and chin. Apparently, I got hotter than I thought walking in.

I arch my shoulders forward, which opens my jacket a little. More steam flows out. I tilt my head down and blow lightly into my jacket. The steam billows out, and it feels warm on my face.

I sit back, take a deep breath, then slowly let it out. The peace and quiet is so nice that I feel myself sinking into the bench and the tree behind my back. The mornings in a deer stand are truly magical.

Suddenly, I hear a crunch in the woods. My heart jumps. I look at Dad. His eyes grow big.

"What is it?" I mouth quietly.

Dad just raises his shoulders and shakes his head.

Then I hear it again. It's behind us. Something is definitely walking around out there. The rustling of dried leaves makes that clear.

Man, I wish the sun were rising so I could see better.

I look at Dad again. He slowly shakes his head, again confirming he doesn't know what it is. He puts his finger to his lips to make sure I stay quiet.

I squeeze my gun tight. Could this be a doe already?

As each moment passes, more light seeps into the woods. But we still need to rely on our hearing more than our sight. We listen as the sound gets closer and closer. Finally, it's right below us. I'm afraid to turn and look—my movement might spook whatever is down there.

Then I hear the sound change. No more crunching over leaves. Instead, I hear scratching on bark. Whatever it is, it's now *coming up the tree*!

I slide into Dad as far as I can. Just when I think I can't get any closer to him, he puts his arm around me and pulls me in. I can't tell whether he's protecting me or using me as a shield!

He's got to protect *me*—that's his job!

The scratching sound shifts. It's as high up in the tree as we are, but it's behind us, on the other side of the tree. Then a figure appears!

I gasp, and Dad covers my mouth with his glove.

It's only a giant gray squirrel. The second he sees us, he panics, races back down the tree, and bounces through the woods.

I look at Dad with disgust. "That was not cool!" I whisper, maybe a little too loud.

Again, Dad shushes me, but he's laughing under his breath. "I don't think he was going to eat us," he says.

I tilt my head and give Dad "the look."

"Funny!" I say.

Then I hear more leaves rustling. I don't even bother to look this time. I figure it's just that darn squirrel coming back.

But then Dad taps me on my left knee and points in the direction of the sound. To my surprise, I can just make out two deer walking our way.

I freeze. I know deer can see the slightest movement. Dad taught me that.

I watch as the deer stop walking and start eating some twigs off a small tree. It's hard to see in the low light, but it looks like their heads are caught up in some branches.

But then one deer turns its head, and it hits me—those aren't branches. They're antlers. The deer are bucks! And giant bucks!

Moving carefully and slowly, I look at Dad. He's watching the bucks through his binoculars. He pulls them down and leans over to whisper in my ear.

"They are huge. Oh, my goodness! One is a ten-pointer, and the other is a twelve-pointer."

I squint to zoom in on each rack and start counting. Dad is right. The buck on the left has six points on each side, and the other buck has five points on each side.

Dad smiles. "Let's just enjoy this, because you can't shoot them," he reminds me.

I give him a frustrated look. I know I can shoot only a doe during the youth deer season. And I know we will follow the rules, as we always do. But under different circumstances—man, I'd love to be able to shoot one of those giants!

I realize that the morning light is now filling the woods. Just minutes ago, we were in moonlight. Now it's like someone finally turned up the lights. The rising sun is getting this day started, and we are seeing deer as a bonus!

All this new light has clearly awakened the birds. Their chirping and singing now fills the woods.

The new light also has made the woods come alive with color. I can see the brilliant reds and yellows of the fall leaves bursting all around me like a slow-motion fireworks show.

The bucks aren't in any hurry as they eat more twigs and walk toward us. When they get into the little clearing below our stand, they start eating the green grass there. It's so cool to watch them. They have no idea we're here.

Then the ten-pointer lowers his antlers and pokes the twelve-pointer on the side. It clearly hurts or surprises the twelve-pointer, because he jumps a couple of feet away. But then he turns and struts right at the ten-pointer.

They both put their heads down and move toward each other. Their antlers touch, creating a loud click. Next, they shake their antlers together, and the clicking noise echoes through the woods. It's so amazing to hear that sound.

The bucks separate for a moment. Then suddenly, the twelve-pointer charges full power at the ten. Their antlers crash together. The bucks pull away, only to square off and charge again.

Now it's an all-out fight! Their antlers are locked together, and both bucks are pushing like crazy. It gets really loud! They're kicking up leaves and crashing their antlers so hard I think they might break.

I freeze with my eyes and mouth open. I cannot look away!

They go at it for several minutes. The ten-pointer seems to be winning. He keeps pushing the twelve backward. Finally, the twelve pulls away and runs off into the woods. The ten stands there proudly a couple of seconds before he decides to chase after the twelve.

Before I know it, silence fills the air.

Our heads slowly turn, and our propped-open eyes meet.

I shake my head. "Wow! That was one of the coolest things I've ever seen!"

"I did not see that coming!" Dad whispers. "I've witnessed that only one other time. How lucky are we today?"

All I can do is grin. I think Dad is right—we *are* lucky today. I can't wait to find out what luck has in store for us next!

Chapter 5

It's really quiet for a while, but then a flock of geese flies over, honking loudly. I watch them soar in a perfect V formation.

As soon as the V passes overhead, I suddenly hear a noise below. This could be the doe we're looking for!

But it's not. It's two turkeys. They come walking by, eating and pecking at what seems to be anything and everything.

"They are jakes—young boy turkeys," Dad whispers. "Can you see the small beards sticking out of their chests?"

Sure enough, I see their little beards sticking out. The jakes are fun to watch and keep me entertained for a while.

After the turkeys disappear, though, it gets quiet again. And I realize I'm getting a little cold.

I nudge close to Dad, hoping he has some extra heat for me. He reaches his right arm around me and pulls me close. It helps. Not to mention I like it when Dad hugs me. I lay my head against his jacket and snuggle in . . .

"Hey—wake up, sleepyhead."

My eyes open. I don't even remember closing them! I think I fell asleep. But now I feel great!

"Whoops!" I whisper, lifting my head. "How long was I out?"

"About twenty minutes. You must have needed it," Dad whispers back. "But now look over there." He points to my right.

At first, I don't see anything. Then something moves. I sit up and focus closer. It moves again. It's a deer!

"Is it a doe?" I whisper with hope.

"No. It's a small buck," Dad says. I crinkle my face in disappointment. It's cool to see another buck, but I'm here for a big doe. And we haven't seen a single one yet.

Dad reaches down and carefully unzips the backpack. The spike is far enough away that he shouldn't hear the noise. I look over anyway to make sure. He is still eating away and has no idea we are here.

Dad reaches into his backpack and pulls out his silver thermos. When he unscrews the top, steam billows out. He uses the cap as a cup and fills it up with hot chocolate.

"Thanks," I whisper as he hands me the cup.

Next, Dad pulls out a plastic baggie with two sugar donuts. This really is my lucky day. Hot chocolate, donuts, and hunting with my dad—nothing could be better!

The hot chocolate is thick and delicious. It warms me right up. The donut is sweet and tasty. As I enjoy my snack, I keep a close eye on the spike. Who knows—maybe a big doe will show up at any moment too.

As I scan to our left, something catches my eye in an opening way back through the trees. I freeze and focus on the spot. Then I see movement.

I tap Dad's leg and point in the direction. He looks out, then shakes his head. He doesn't see it.

"Out there," I whisper as I point. "I saw something move."

Dad pulls up his binoculars and slowly sweeps them back and forth over the area where I pointed. Then he stops and keeps the binoculars still.

"Gotcha!" he says. "I see it—it's a doe! Good eye, Crystal!"

I feel so proud that I saw the deer before Dad!

"She needs to come in closer for you to get a shot. Let's see what happens," Dad says.

With new hope, I keep my eyes peeled in her direction. I see movement every once in a while, but she's not budging. I'm getting frustrated.

After what seems like forever, she simply disappears. We never see her again.

Now I'm beyond frustrated. What happened to our luck?

Dad looks at his watch. "It's ten forty-five. Are you ready to head in for some bacon and eggs?"

I frown a little as I think it over. I know this is how it usually works with deer hunting. Deer are most active around dawn and dusk, so most hunters just go out in the morning and the evening. So, it's probably best to head back to the cabin and get something to eat. Our chances of seeing a deer now would be slim.

I get all that. Still . . . I don't love coming up empty-handed on my very first morning of hunting!

"I suppose we can head in," I finally say. "I guess I am getting hungry. But I really wanted to get a deer this morning!"

Dad gives me a reassuring smile. "I know you did—I did too! But don't you worry. We'll come back out for the evening hunt. And we have tomorrow morning. You still have time!"

I nod and smile back. I feel a little better. Maybe.

Dad texts Greg to meet us on the road as I carefully unload my gun so we can safely climb down out of the stand. We make our way down the trail and back to the truck, then go pick up Greg and Megan.

All the way back to the cabin, Megan can't stop talking about her hunt. They saw a six-pointer, two grouse, a red squirrel, and a gray squirrel. They also saw two does, but each had a fawn with her, so they passed on them.

As she shares her tales, Megan is as fired up as I've ever seen her. Just listening to her fires me up as well. I may be disappointed that I didn't get a doe, but I really did have a great time this morning.

Extra excited now, I tell Greg and Megan about all the action we saw on our side: the gray squirrel that "attacked" us, the two giant bucks fighting, the geese, the jakes, the spike buck, and the disappearing doe. Megan and Greg can't believe it. They're especially amazed that we got to watch those two bucks sparring.

"Man, I hope to see those bucks," Greg says. "I've never laid eyes on bucks that big!"

"That's one thing that makes hunting so fun," Dad says. "You get to see so many different critters—not just the ones you're hunting."

He looks at me in the rearview mirror and winks. I grin right back.

Doe or no doe, I'm definitely hooked on hunting!

Chapter 6

Dad and Greg whip us up a batch of scrambled eggs and maple venison bacon. The smell of the maple bacon fills the cabin and my nose. I can't wait to shoot a deer so I can have some bacon made out of *my* deer.

We won't go back out hunting until late afternoon. So to pass some time, Megan and I hop on our four-wheeler. We love four-wheeling. For over an hour, we cruise on the trails around the cabin, then head back inside to take a much-needed nap. Megan especially loves to catch some extra Zs!

Dad wakes me up around 3:30 and says it's time to get ready for the evening hunt. It doesn't take me long to come to life. I nudge Megan to wake her up too.

Soon we're in our hunting clothes, piled into the truck, and heading back to the hunting land.

"Oh yeah—tonight's the night! I can feel it," Megan says. "Crystal, are you feeling lucky?"

"I just hope we get to see something," I reply. "It's so much fun watching animals in the woods. Even if I don't get a doe."

"Yeah, good point," Megan says. After a second, she adds, "But I still want to get a deer!"

We drop off Megan and Greg, and they start walking back to Uncle Vern's

Stand. Then Dad and I keep driving, heading for the spot where we parked this morning. From here, we'll once again walk back to Dad's stand.

We make our way slowly through the woods, with Dad leading and me following behind. About halfway down the trail, he stops in his tracks so fast that I collide into him. He puts his arm around me and points into the woods.

"Look what's lying on top of that tree stump!" he whispers into my ear.

I cannot believe my eyes. It's a red fox curled up and sound asleep! I turn to Dad and shake my head in awe.

"Let's see how close we can get to him," Dad whispers.

I'm not too sure about this plan, but I figure I'll follow Dad's lead as he steps off the trail and into the woods. One careful step at a time, we narrow the distance to that sleepyhead.

When we're closer than I ever dreamed you could get to a sleeping fox, his ear twitches. We freeze. Then he raises his head and looks right at us.

If there's ever a time for a fox's eyes to pop out of his head, this is it. The fox almost does a backflip when he realizes two people are standing just a few steps away from him. He bolts through the woods and is gone in a flash.

"That was amazing!" I whisper. "Have you ever seen that before, Dad?"

"Never. I can't believe we got so close! He must have been dreaming about chasing rabbits or something."

"Dreaming about rabbits?" I repeat. I tilt my head and give him the look.

I shake my head at Dad's silly comment as we go back to the trail and continue our walk. Then I can't stop thinking about animals dreaming. I wonder if that fox *does* dream. I wonder what a deer would dream about. Crazy stuff to think about that's for sure.

Then I see Dad's magical deer stand. Time to focus on seeing deer rather than thinking about what they might be dreaming about. We climb up and settle in.

Once again, I'm ready for action!

A little red squirrel comes running by. Instead of crunching through leaves, he manages to stay pretty quiet by hopping on branches lying on the ground. A good trick to keep him undetected from that sleepyhead fox.

To test out my scope, I pull my gun up and find the little guy through the eyepiece. Keeping my crosshairs right on him, I follow him as he darts about.

Oh man, I'm ready for a deer! My gun feels perfect, and my scope is crystal clear.

"Bring on a big doe," I whisper to Dad as I set my gun back down. "I bet one will come out any second now!"

"Maybe . . ." Dad whispers back. "But maybe not too. Things might be a little slow this afternoon. Deer don't move around a lot at this time of day. We likely won't see much action until dusk sets in."

I crinkle my eyebrows. "Then why are we out here now? Why don't we wait until it's closer to dusk?"

"The goal is to be in the stand early, long before the deer start moving. That way, we won't scare them off. They can see and hear us. They can even smell our scent from our boots on the trail! So the longer we're up in the stand, the better." He pats my shoulder. "Being patient and putting in our time are part of deer hunting."

I nod up and down as I process what Dad just said. He sure does know a lot about hunting!

Even though we likely won't see deer right now, I'm still determined to keep my eyes and ears sharp. Like a hawk, I keep scanning the woods, searching for any movement. The minutes tick by, one after another. But no signs of deer. No signs of anything, for that matter.

Then it seems like the minutes are stretching into hours. I'm determined to stay patient and wait this out. But after a while, I can't help but sigh quietly and turn to Dad for some encouragement.

With a little smile, he pulls out his cell phone and a set of earbuds. "Here. You get one, and I get one."

I put the earbud in my left ear while Dad puts his in his right. Then my favorite Taylor Swift song comes on!

I look at Dad in amazement. One, I can't believe it's Taylor Swift. Two, I'm surprised he even knows how to play music on a phone!

Dad grins and winks. He clearly thinks he's cool.

"I like her songs too," he whispers into my other ear.

This is awesome. I'm listening to my favorite music while keeping my eyes peeled for deer. It's the best of both worlds.

After several songs, Dad stops the music and slides the earbuds out of my ear and his.

"The sun is below the trees now," he whispers. "That means we have about an hour left of light. This is prime time for the deer to move. Get ready—it could happen at any time."

I give him a thumbs-up. That's good news to hear.

I check out the sun's position. Dad's right. It is down in the trees. Sunbeams pierce through the forest like a bunch of flashlights. The daylight is slowly melting from the sky.

Then my heart jumps—I hear leaves crunching to my right. What could that be?

I'm totally shocked to see what's coming our way. It is a giant black wolf!

I quickly look at Dad. I'm sure my wide eyes give away just how scared I am.

"It's OK," he reassures me. "We're safe up here. Just sit and watch him. Not everyone gets to see a wolf!"

Despite his reassurance, I still scoot closer to him as we watch the wolf together.

The wolf's legs and tail are so long. He lopes into our opening, then abruptly stops. His ears perk up and turn forward. He looks down into the grass, then pounces and sticks his nose in.

When he pulls up, he doesn't have anything in his mouth. But it's clear he thought something was there in the grass. Something tasty.

This is amazing!

Next, he cocks his head and freezes, just like our dog, Trigger, does when I'm holding a treat. Quickly, the wolf turns to his right. He jumps up, then sticks his nose down into the grass again. He pushes his nose through the grass as if he were a vacuum cleaner. When he pulls it up, he still has nothing.

He starts going crazy now, looking left, then right. He can definitely smell something in the grass. He hops from spot to spot, diving after whatever is down there.

Finally, he makes a big leap to his left and dives in again. This time, he comes up with a big brown mouse hanging from his mouth.

He shakes the mouse like a rag doll. And then with one quick motion, he opens his mouth and gobbles the mouse up.

I crinkle my nose. Gross!

My face relaxes, though, when I realize what I just saw with my own eyes, in real life. I got to see a wolf catch dinner—or at least a snack.

Then the wolf freezes and puts his nose into the air. I can tell he's trying to smell something. I figure another mouse.

But I'm wrong.

As if we'd called out to him and said, "Hey, we're up here!" he turns and looks right into my eyes.

Like a clamp, my hand squeezes Dad's knee.

Now that the wolf knows he's not alone, he crouches low, turns, and slithers quickly into the woods.

I slowly turn my head and look at Dad. His face is beaming with excitement.

"Wasn't that amazing?" he whispers.

"That wolf looked right into my eyes!" I gush. "He knew we were here!"

"Yep. He smelled us. They have an amazing sense of smell."

I take a deep breath in, then slowly let it out to calm down. "That was so cool—and very scary at the same time."

But then another thought crosses my mind.

"Oh, man—we eventually have to get out of this tree. He won't wait for us down there or anything, will he?"

"Absolutely not," Dad answers. "He's way more scared of us than we are of him."

"Speak for yourself. I think I have him beat."

I settle back down and look around to get my bearings. I realize the light in the woods is really fading now. No more sunbeams. Now just a warm glow fills the woods. And not a breath of air. We should be able to hear a deer crunching in the leaves from a long way off. I'm hoping I hear that crunching soon.

As if on cue, I instantly hear noise. It gets louder, and I try to focus on where it's coming from. I finally realize I'm hearing not just leaves crunching but animals running. Big animals. This is no squirrel or fox. Not even a wolf.

Four deer come racing by!

Chapter 7

I grab my gun and get it ready. The deer keep running but finally stop way back in the woods. Two of them slip farther back into the forest, disappearing. But I can still see the other two.

"They are both big does," Dad says with his binoculars up to his eyes.

"Should I take the one on the left? I can see her clearly," I say with excitement.

"Sure. Why not give it a try? Turn and rest your gun on the railing so you can hold steady," he instructs.

Oh my gosh. Is this it? Is this actually happening?

I quickly slide back and turn my body. The movement makes the seat creak and my boots squeak.

I cringe. That was *way* too loud.

Sure enough, both deer turn and look right at us. They're on full alert. Their ears and tails are straight up. I expect them to bolt any second. But to my surprise, the doe on the left starts marching slowly right at us.

"Don't move," Dad whispers as quietly as he can. "She's trying to figure out what made that noise."

The doe stops. She stands as still as a statue for a second, then she stomps her right hoof. It's really loud. Next, she lets out an amazing noise—it sounds like she's blowing into a huge broken whistle. It startles me!

"That's a warning sound, a snort," Dad whispers from behind me. "It lets the other animals know something's not right." His whisper is filled with anticipation. "Let's wait and see what happens!"

After a few seconds, the doe starts walking again. She's marching even closer to us now.

My heart beats faster. My hands shake. My whole body trembles.

"Relax and breathe," Dad says. He puts his hand on my back and squeezes softly.

That helps me calm down a little.

Now the big doe is about twenty steps away and still staring right up at us. She stomps her hoof and makes that loud whistle again. Then she turns and leaps three times to the right with her white tail wagging and pointing high.

My heart nearly bursts with both excitement and disappointment. Is she leaving?

But no—she suddenly stops.

"If you can get on her, you can take the shot now!" Dad says in an urgent whisper.

I didn't expect to hear that! *This is it!*

In a bit of a panic, I shift around to get in position—but I end up slipping right off the bench. So now I have to squat as I try my best to look through my scope. The whole time, I'm making all kinds of noise, and I'm sure the doe can see me moving.

She lets out one more whistle, then leaps back into the woods. All I can see is her white tail flashing through the trees as she runs to catch up to the other deer.

I didn't even have enough time to turn my safety off.

I stand up and let out a big sigh. "Ugh!"

"Well, that was exciting!" Dad says with a big smile.

"*Exciting?*" I repeat. "What do you mean? I made way too much noise!" My head hangs down. "I'm sorry, Dad."

"Don't be sorry one bit," he says, putting a hand on my shoulder. "It takes a lot of practice to learn how to be silent in a deer stand."

"But that was my chance!" I insist.

"One of the many things you'll learn about hunting is that sometimes it just doesn't work out. But other times, it does. You just have to keep trying. I've messed up on more deer than you could imagine. It's the way I've learned how to be a better hunter. Each time you learn something."

I nod and manage a bit of a smile. It's good to hear this is all part of hunting.

"And don't forget," Dad adds, "we still have tomorrow. This wasn't your last chance. Your luck may change tomorrow. In fact, it can change in a moment! As hunters, we have to be patient and persistent."

Suddenly, a gunshot rings out. I jump.

Dad looks at me with a happy grin. "That could be Megan! Let me text Greg to see."

He slips his phone out of his pocket and texts a message to Greg. We hold our breath, looking down at his phone, waiting for a reply.

Then a reply pops up. *Doe down!*

We both look at each other and high-five.

"That's awesome!" I say, beaming with excitement for my best friend. "Megan said she felt lucky tonight. I can't wait to see the smile on her face!"

"Me too! Let's get over there and check it out!"

Chapter 8

We make our way back to the truck just as the day gives into the night. We drive to the other side of the property, where Greg and Megan are waiting for us. As the headlights shine on Megan, she's waving her arms up and doing a silly dance.

"Someone looks happy," Dad says.

Before Dad even gets the truck in park, I jump out as fast as I can. I run to Megan and give her a big hug.

Megan starts singing. "Oh yeah, oh yeah—I got my deer!" The song goes well with her dance.

Dad walks up and gives her a high five. "Way to go, Megan! That sounds like a first deer cheer to me." He then turns to Greg. "Where is it?"

"Not far from the stand. I'm hoping you can give me a hand dragging her out."

"Sounds good to me," Dad replies. "Let's go get her!"

We put our headlamps on and follow Greg back to the stand. The whole way there, Megan can't stop talking about how excited she is. Once we reach the stand, she launches into the story.

"OK, OK—let me explain how this happened," she begins, talking a mile a minute. "Obviously, Dad and I were sitting up there."

She points to the stand.

"Then out of nowhere, the doe just appeared! I think we were both daydreaming at the time. I'm not sure. But for whatever reason, we didn't see her walk in. Then I happened to look out and couldn't believe my eyes. There she was! I elbowed Dad in the side, and he made a noise. That could have blown the whole thing! But it didn't."

I see Dad and Greg exchange little smiles.

"Then I got my gun ready," Megan continues, not slowing down a bit. "My heart was pounding out of my chest. Oh, my goodness—I was freaking out! Dad told me to take a few breaths to calm down. I did, and it helped. Well, a little. I was still kind of freaking out."

Now it's my turn to exchange smiles with Dad. Megan's story sounds a lot like mine. I'm glad I'm not the only one who panicked.

"The doe walked over by that big oak tree," Megan says. "Well, Dad said it's an oak. I have no idea. It's that one, over there."

She points out toward a tree, though it's way too dark to see anything beyond the beam of our headlamps.

"And then the doe stopped!" Her voice is very dramatic now. "I set my gun on the railing, clicked my safety off, and put the crosshairs right behind her shoulder."

She turns to me.

"Crystal, it was just like our dads have told us a hundred times. 'Put the crosshairs right behind the shoulder.'" She makes her voice deep to sound like a dad. "Dad was even saying that as I lined up the shot. Then I squeezed the trigger! The gun didn't even scare me a bit. The deer jumped up like a rabbit and ran right over there."

She points off into the woods again. For as fast as she's talking and as long as this story is, I'm not sure how Megan isn't out of breath yet.

"I freaked out for a little bit, and my hands were shaking like crazy. Then once I stopped freaking out, Dad and I hugged a bunch, then we climbed down. Dad found the blood trail, and we followed it. Just like professional hunters. 'Cause you know, that's what we are—professional hunters. We followed the blood, and the deer was lying right over there." More pointing. "She didn't go very far at all."

Megan suddenly stops and takes a gulping breath.

"And *that's* how it all happened!"

Greg and Dad look at each other again.

"Did you get all that?" Greg says with his eyes wide open. He clearly looks like someone who took in a little too much information.

"I sure did," Dad says. "And I think she's still freaking out!"

We all laugh, even Megan.

"All right, Miss Professional Hunter— let's go see this deer," Dad says, still laughing.

We follow Megan and Greg off into the woods. Sure enough, there's a big doe lying there. Megan can't stop smiling and talking. She's so proud of this deer.

And I'm so proud of her. This really is a great moment!

Dad takes a bunch of pictures. Pictures of Megan. Pictures of Megan and Greg. Pictures of me and Megan. Just about every combo we can imagine.

When Dad finally puts his phone away, I give Megan one more big hug.

"Great job!" I tell her. "You did it!"

"Crystal, girl," she says, pointing at me, "tomorrow is *your* day. You're gonna get your deer tomorrow. I just know it!"

Her confidence makes me feel good and gives me new hope.

If she can do it, I can too!

Chapter 9

It's a late night by the time we get back and eat dinner. After a few more stories from Megan, we hit the sack. I'm exhausted—but also eager for what tomorrow will bring.

Before I know it, Dad's wake-up nudge comes as a surprise.

"Good morning, sweet pea," he whispers so he doesn't also wake up Megan. "Time to get up. This could be your lucky day."

I smile, letting the words sink in. Dad is so good at keeping me fired up.

"It already *is* my lucky day, Dad. That's because I get to go hunting with you!" I whisper with a warm smile.

"I think *I'm* the lucky one," he says, giving me a wink.

I eat a bowl of Cinnamon Toast Crunch, my favorite cereal. The best part is drinking the milk at the end. I drop my bowl off at the sink and then go get dressed. Soon, we're out the door and hopping in the truck.

As we head for the hunting land, I think about Megan. Man, I want to get a deer and feel that excitement too! I'm thrilled and nervous at the same time. Today's the last day of the youth hunt. My last chance.

Now or never.

Once we park and get out of the truck, I look up. There are a billion stars out. I take a deep breath of cool air. It's cold enough this morning to see my breath in the moonlight.

It's magical being up this early. It's so quiet and peaceful.

I stay close to Dad as we make our way down the path. The full moon seems to follow us.

Once we get to the stand, it takes a bit to get settled in. But then it's perfectly quiet. The only thing I can hear is my own breath going in and out of my nose.

Suddenly, something breaks the silence. It's an owl hooting. Soon another joins in.

"Those are great horned owls," Dad whispers.

"*Who who, who who, who who, who whooooo?*" the owls say. It sounds like a question.

"I don't know who!" Dad jokes. "Why do they keep asking?"

I just shake my head and roll my eyes.

The colors of the woods start to glow. This is magical too—to watch the leaves go from a colorless gray to bold reds, yellows, and greens in minutes. I love the fall colors!

I keep my eyes and ears on full alert, hoping to sense a deer. Nothing's moving below us yet this morning. Not even a squirrel.

A crow flies over, and her call echoes through the woods. Then I catch movement in front of us. Before I can blink, an owl flies in and lands in the tree next to us. She doesn't even make a sound!

The owl faces away from us. Then she turns her head all the way around and looks right at me. It's like her head is on a swivel. It's so cool. I cannot believe how big and beautiful she is.

I look at Dad and give him my crazy-face look, the one that says, "This is unbelievable!"

He nods his head up and down, agreeing with me.

Then the owl turns around on the branch. She seems to be looking at something down below, in the clearing.

Suddenly, she tips forward and spreads out her giant wings. Like a torpedo, she shoots to the ground.

At the last second, her legs and talons spring forward. The dried leaves rustle and scatter as she hits the ground. When she lifts up her right foot, she has a big brown mouse in her talons.

She turns her head and looks up at us. Maybe she's proud to show us that she caught a mouse. Or maybe she wants us to know she's not happy that we're interrupting her breakfast. Either way, she jumps up and flies silently through the trees, with the mouse in her talons.

"Just like on National Geographic," Dad says.

"That was amazing!" I add.

First, a wolf. Now, an owl. How lucky are we to see these great hunters in action!

Suddenly, I hear something crunching back in the woods. I look at Dad, and he looks at me.

Could this be the deer I've been waiting for?

My ears zero in on the sound, but I don't see anything yet. I keep my head still so I can catch any movement. Then the sound stops.

I look at Dad, worried.

"Be patient," he whispers. "I think that's a deer."

I keep listening. Soon the *crunch-crunch* starts up again. Eventually, I can tell the crunches are footsteps in the leaves. And they're getting closer. My heart pounds with excitement.

I catch movement. A flash.

I tap Dad's knee.

"Yep, I saw it too," he whispers.

A figure finally appears. It's a deer walking right to us, down the main runway. Another one appears behind it. Two deer!

Then my heart sinks. It's just those two giant bucks from yesterday morning.

I frown at Dad. Who would believe it could be *unlucky* to see two huge bucks? But I'm after a big doe.

The two giants walk right across the shooting lane. That's an area Dad clears out every spring. He cuts down small trees and clears out brush that could block a shot from our stand. Dad takes a lot of pride in how well he clears the shooting lane. I'm thankful he does such a good job because it makes it a lot easier to see the deer.

Eventually, the two big guys walk right into our opening below the stand and start eating. They are beautiful. I watch in amazement as they mill around, only steps below us.

Suddenly, the twelve struts over to the ten. He puts his head down, and they click antlers.

I slowly shake my head. Are they really going to fight again?

They click their antlers a few more times. But then they stop. It's like they're bored.

The twelve gets back on the runway and walks past us. The ten follows behind. Soon, they're both out of sight.

"Wow," Dad says. "I'm definitely sitting here next weekend with my bow. I can't wait!"

I nod, remembering that it's actually bow season right now. In fact, Dad left his bow home this weekend so he could take me out for the youth hunt. It's pretty cool that he did that just for me.

Because Dad loves hunting more than anyone else I know, I hope he does get one of those giant bucks next weekend. That would be awesome.

I'm daydreaming about Dad getting one of those bucks when I hear footsteps again. When I look out, I see three deer to our right, walking our way. They're in really thick brush, so I catch only glimpses of them.

Dad has his binoculars up and is watching them. "There's a mom and fawn in the front," he whispers. "But the third is a big doe without a fawn."

He lowers the binoculars and looks right at me.

"That's your deer!"

Chapter 10

"Really?" I ask, my eyes wide.

"Yep," he says. "Get your gun ready. They're gonna cross the shooting lane."

My heart pounds like a drum. This is really happening!

I know I need to be quieter this time as I get into position. I carefully raise my gun and set the barrel on the wood railing. Then I crouch down as silently as I can until I can see through my scope perfectly. I might be in stealth mode, but my hands still shake as I try to hold my gun steady.

"Calm down—it's OK," Dad whispers. He must see me shaking. "Take a long, deep breath, and let it out slowly. That will help your hands."

I suck in a big breath through my nose and let it out slowly. It does help calm me down. I take another breath and let it out too. My hands aren't quite so bad now. As long as I hold my gun barrel down to the wood railing, I'll be able to make a good shot.

I'm pretty sure, anyway.

The deer are moving our way slowly, eating as they go. I wait and watch like a lion in the grass. With every breath, I feel calmer. I'm ready for action!

Minutes go by. One slow step at a time, the deer are heading toward the shooting lane. They're sure taking their time.

Meanwhile, I'm going crazy. I want them to get to the shooting lane *now*, so I can get a shot.

Finally, the first doe and her fawn enter the lane. They start eating the green grass. Then the big single doe walks out behind them. I can tell she's the one.

"You want the one in the back," Dad confirms. "But the other two are blocking your shot. Hang tight."

Looking through my scope, I can see all three deer perfectly. But Dad's right. The big doe is totally blocked by the fawn.

Then the fawn takes a few steps forward.

"You're clear!" Dad whispers a little louder. "Take her when you're ready!"

With one more deep breath, I click off my safety and line up the crosshairs right behind the doe's front shoulder. I squeeze the trigger.

BOOM!

The gun goes off. It kicks up instantly, and I lose sight of the deer.

"Yes!" Dad exclaims. "You got her! A perfect shot!"

I quickly look over the scope. To my amazement, the big doe is lying right where I shot her.

"You dropped her in her tracks! Woo-hoo!" Dad howls.

Now I think *he's* the one freaking out!

Even though we're both excited, I suddenly remember to click my safety back on. Then with trembling hands, I prop my gun in the corner.

"Good thinking—way to be safe," Dad says.

I'm proud of myself for remembering the safety steps. It makes me shine even more with a smile.

When I stand and turn to Dad, he gives me a high five that just about knocks my hand off. Then he gives me such a big hug that it lifts me right off my feet. He sets me on the bench, and we both raise our hands up in victory.

"You did it!" Dad says, beaming. "You got your first deer. And what a great shot!"

I just stand there, hugging Dad and grinning like crazy. This is an amazing feeling. Victory for sure!

"Let's get down and go check her out!" Dad says.

We climb down, and I run over to the deer. She is big and perfect. Dad gives me a double high five this time. This is so cool!

Of course, Dad takes a bunch of pictures of me with my deer. Then we decide to head back to get Greg and Megan. I can't wait to tell Megan every detail. She's going to freak out!

I feel like I'm floating the whole drive to the cabin. This has been one of the best weekends of my life. My first deer. But not my last.

I can't wait to go hunting again!

About the Author

Kevin Lovegreen was born and raised in Minnesota, where he lives with his loving wife and two amazing children. Hunting, fishing, and the outdoors have always been a big part of his life. From chasing squirrels as a child to chasing elk as an adult, Kevin loves the thrill of hunting. But even more, he loves telling the stories of the adventure. Presenting at schools and connecting with kids about the outdoors is one of his favorite things to do.

www.KevinLovegreen.com

Other Books in the Series

AR-rated
(Accelerated Reader)

Award-winning

To order books or learn about
school visits please go to
www.KevinLovegreen.com

A note to the reader,

All the stories in the Lucky Luke's Adventures series are based on real experiences that happened to me or my family.

If you like the book, please help spread the word by telling all your friends!

>Thanks for reading!
>Kevin Lovegreen